Skip Through the Seasons

To Cecilia — S. B.

To Mum and Dad — M. C.

Barefoot Books
124 Walcot Street
Bath BA1 5BG

This book was typeset in Syntax Black and Jacoby ICG Black
The illustrations were prepared in gouache and paper collage

Graphic design by Barefoot Books, Bath. Colour separation by Bright Arts, Singapore
Printed and bound in China by Printplus Ltd

This book has been printed on 100% acid-free paper

Paperback ISBN 1-905236-70-0

British Cataloguing-in-Publication Data: a catalogue
record for this book is available from the British Library

5 7 9 8 6 4

Skip through the Seasons

written by

Stella Blackstone

illustrated by

Maria Carluccio

Barefoot Books
Celebrating Art and Story

Jump into **January**, come along with me!

teddy bear   hoods   footprints   puck   smoke   earmuffs

The local pond is glazed with ice — what can you see?

pine trees   skates   pipe   hockey stick   dog   house

Fly into **February**, come along with me!

skis   carrot   snowball   snowman   sledge   ski poles

The hillside glistens, white with snow — what can you see?

snow boots   *jacket*   **goggles**   *mittens*   **rabbit**   *bird*

Whirl into **March**, come along with me!

church   dog   truck   bicycle   frisbee   hats

The wind is whistling down the street — what can you see?

leaves   kite   car   clothes-line   flag   parcel

Splash into **April**,
come along with me!

boots   puddles   umbrellas   fountain   cat   pavement

The first spring rains are sweet and warm
— what can you see?

rain hats   steps   drainpipe   paper boat   gate   daffodils

Move into **May**, come along with me!

aprons　　hoe　　flower pots　　trolley　　rakes　　cherry blossom

It's time to make our gardens grow
— what can you see?

sprinkler   hoses   trowel   watering can   fork   seed trays

Race into **June**, come along with me!

scooter   thermos   picnic rug   basket   butterfly   swing

It's so much fun to eat outdoors
— what can you see?

skateboard   bread   bicycle   bananas   cooler   picnic bench

Jive into **July**, come along with me!

juggler   dolls   dodgem cars   ice cream stand   candy floss

The fair is full of games and rides — what can you see?

carousel   balloons   flags   ticket booth   ferris wheel   moon

Sail into **August**,
come along with me!

sailboats   buckets   fisherman   crab   beach ball   sunglasses

The sand is soft, the sea is warm — what can you see?

spade   seagull   hammock   surfboard   sandcastles   flippers

Slide into **September,**
come along with me!

bus   teacher   lunch boxes   book   skipping rope   football

It's time to go to school again
— what can you see?

backpacks   poster   slide   hopscotch   hula hoop   squirrel

Twirl into **October**,
come along with me!

donkey beehive baskets tyre swing apples plums

The orchard trees are full of fruit
— what can you see?

pears   pumpkins   wheelbarrow   bucket   ladder   sheep

Sweep into **November**,
come along with me!

bonfire   rake   birdhouse   shutters   lantern   spectacles

The leaves are dancing as they fall
— what can you see?

overcoat   cat   piano   tree house   sack   broom

Dance into **December**,
come along with me!

candles   party lights   glasses   streamers   drum   presents

Let's celebrate the turning year,
and everything we see.

cakes   poinsettia   stockings   candy canes   saxophone   bottles

All Around the Calendar

Now that you've travelled all around the changing year, find out where the names of the months come from:

April – from the Latin word aperire, meaning 'to open'

January – named after Janus, Roman god of doorways and beginnings

May – named after Maia, Roman goddess of spring

February – named after Februa, Roman festival of purification

June – named after Juno, Roman goddess of marriage

March – named after Mars, Roman god of war

July – named after Julius Caesar, Roman general and dictator

August – named after Augustus, Roman emperor

October – from the Latin word octo meaning 'eight' (October was the eighth month of the earliest Roman calendar)

September – from the Latin word septem, meaning 'seven' (September was the seventh month of the earliest Roman calendar)

November – from the Latin word novem, meaning 'nine' (November was the ninth month of the earliest Roman calendar)

You'll notice a Roman influence – that's because our calendar (365 days in the year, with an extra day added every fourth year) was introduced by the Roman Dictator, Julius Caesar, in AD 45. The Romans brought their calendar to the countries they conquered and over the centuries it became adopted by different cultures across the world.

December – from the Latin word decem, meaning 'ten' (December was the tenth month of the earliest Roman calendar)

The Changing Seasons

The year is divided into four seasons — spring, summer, autumn and winter. But what makes these seasons? Each year the Earth travels once around the sun. The seasons are defined by the Earth's position on this journey — or orbit.

While the Earth travels around the sun, it also spins on its axis. It takes the Earth one day to rotate completely. The Earth is tilted on its axis. This causes the North Pole to be tilted towards the Sun for half of the year, and the South Pole to be tilted towards the Sun for the other half of the year. The hemisphere that is tilted towards the Sun has a longer day and receives more of the Sun's rays than the hemisphere that is tilted away. Therefore, the hemisphere that is closest to the Sun at any given time is experiencing summer.

If the Earth's axis was not tilted, each night and day everywhere on Earth would always be twelve hours long and we would have no seasons!

The Calendar

Calendars are a system of keeping track of time. They divide time into days, weeks, months and years. There have been many different calendars throughout the ages:

Babylonian – a calendar of twelve lunar months of thirty days each. The Babylonians added extra months when necessary to keep the calendar in line with the seasons.

Ancient Egyptian – the first to replace the lunar calendar (determined by the moon phases) with a calendar based on the solar year (determined by the sun). Each week was ten days long.

Roman – the original Roman calendar had ten months, with 304 days in a year. The year began with March.

Aztec – each week was only five days long, each month was four weeks long.

Gregorian – in 1582 Pope Gregory introduced a new calendar that adjusted the leap years so that time ran more smoothly. This evolved into the calendar we know today.

Hebrew – a lunar calendar divided into twelve months of twenty-nine or thirty days each. The year is about 354 days long. The result of this is that the entire year moves eleven or twelve days per year. An additional month is added about every three years to compensate for this shift.

Islamic – the Islamic year consists of twelve lunar months, and its starting point is AD 622, the day after the Hegira, or the emigration of Muhammad from Mecca to Medina.

Hindu – a lunar calendar that dates from 3101 BC. The year is divided into twelve lunar months in accordance with the signs of the zodiac. The months vary in length from twenty-nine to thirty-two days.

Days of the Week

English	French	Spanish	Italian	German	Anglo-Saxon
Sunday	dimanche	domingo	domenica	Sonntag	Sunnandaeg
Monday	lundi	lunes	lunedi	Montag	Monandaeg
Tuesday	mardi	martes	martedi	Dienstag	Tiwesdaeg
Wednesday	mercredi	miércoles	mercoledi	Mittwoch	Wodneesdaeg
Thursday	jeudi	jueves	giovedi	Donnerstag	Thuresdaeg
Friday	vendredi	viernes	venerdi	Freitag	Frigedaeg
Saturday	samedi	sábado	sabato	Samstag	Saeternesdaeg

Most of the French, Spanish and Italian names for the days of the week are close to the Roman names for the gods and planets. The English and German names are closer to those of the Norse gods. For example, Donner means thunder, so that Thursday is the 'day of thunder' — the mark of the great god Thor.

Deities of the Week

Day	Planet	Babylonian	Greek	Roman	Norse
Sunday	Sun	Shamash	Helios/Apollo	Mithras	Sunna
Monday	Moon	Sin	Selene/Artemis	Diana	Sinhtgunt
Tuesday	Mars	Nergal	Ares	Mars	Tiw
Wednesday	Mercury	Nabu	Hermes	Mercury	Woden/Odin
Thursday	Jupiter	Marduk	Zeus	Jupiter	Thor
Friday	Venus	Ishtar	Aphrodite	Venus	Freya
Saturday	Saturn	Ninurta/Ninib	Cronus	Saturn	(Saturn)